Foxwood Tales

present the story of
Harvey, Rue and Willy in . . .

For William

Scholastic Children's Books,
Scholastic Publications Ltd,
7-9 Pratt Street, London NW1 0AE, UK

Scholastic Inc.,
730 Broadway, New York, NY 10003, USA

Scholastic Canada Ltd,
123 Newkirk Road, Richmond Hill,
Ontario, Canada L4C 3G5

Ashton Scholastic Pty Ltd,
P O Box 579, Gosford, New South Wales,
Australia

Ashton Scholastic Ltd,
Private Bag 1, Penrose, Auckland,
New Zealand

First published in the UK by André Deutsch Children's Books 1988
Reprinted 1989
Reprinted by Scholastic Publications Ltd, 1992

Text copyright © 1988 by Cynthia Paterson
Illustrations copyright © 1988 by Brian Paterson

ISBN 0 590 54067 X

Printed in Hong Kong by Paramount Printing Group Ltd.

The Foxwood Surprise

Written and illustrated by
Cynthia and Brian Paterson

André Deutsch Children's Books
Scholastic Children's Books
London

'Is Harvey at home?' asked Willy Hedgehog, kicking snow from his wellingtons.

'He's upstairs with Rue,' said Mrs Mouse. 'Go and see what they're up to, Willy. They're making an awful noise.'

'There you are, Willy,' said Rue as Willy opened the door. 'And about time. We've finished our toboggans and nearly done yours.'

'Thanks,' said Willy. 'But I haven't been wasting my time. I've done our Christmas present list.'

'Don't talk about Christmas presents,' groaned Harvey. 'We've no money left. You know how much the stuff for the toboggans cost.'

'Let's earn some, then,' said Willy.

'How?' asked Harvey and Rue together.

'Carol singing?' suggested Willy. 'It's Christmas, isn't it?'

'I can't sing for toffee,' muttered Rue.

'Not toffee, money.' Willy could never resist a joke.

'Oh, shut up, Willy,' snapped Rue. 'This is no time for feeble jokes.'

Willy was just about to answer when Harvey stopped him. 'Carol singing's not a bad idea, Willy,' he said. 'Let's start tonight.'

That evening, well wrapped up and carrying lanterns and sheets of music, the three friends met outside Mr Gruffey's shop. It was shut.

'He's locked up early because of the snow,' said Rue, reading a note pinned to the door.

'There's plenty more places,' said Willy cheerfully. 'Let's try Mrs Mole next.'

But Mrs Mole's house was in darkness, and so were the next three houses they tried. By the time they got to Mrs Squirrel's they were almost ready to give up.

'What shall we sing first?' said Willy, shuffling the sheets in his hand.

'That's just it,' said Harvey. 'We're not organised. We don't know what to sing and we don't know who's at home. You shouldn't have been in such a hurry, Willy.'

'I wasn't,' shouted Willy. 'You were the one who wanted to start tonight.'

The window above them flew open. 'Stop that noise,' called Mrs Squirrel. 'You'll wake my babies.'

'That settles it,' said Harvey. 'The first house with someone at home and she tells us to shut up. I'm going home.'

'Hang on,' said Willy. 'Don't go yet. I've got a brilliant idea.'

'Not another one,' said Rue. He shrugged. 'Well, let's hear it.'

'It's the new squire at the Old Manor House,' said Willy. 'Squire Fox. Everyone says he's very rich.'

'That's right,' said Harvey, seeing Willy's idea. 'Dad says he's rolling in it.'

'Rolling in what?' asked Rue. He had no idea what Harvey and Willy were talking about.

'Money, you fool,' said Willy. 'If we play our cards right we might get all we need from him.'

'Unless he's out . . .' muttered Rue.

'It's worth a try,' insisted Willy.

Half an hour later they reached the Manor House. 'I hope you're right, Willy,' said Harvey doubtfully, untying the rusty chain round the gates. 'It looks deserted to me.'

Willy wasn't listening. 'Some place,' he muttered, holding the lantern high. 'You'd have to be rich to live in a house like this.'

'It gives me the creeps,' said Rue.

They climbed the steps to the front
door and Rue banged the brass knocker loudly.

'Let's get started,' said Willy. 'And sing up, so they can hear us.'

They were heard all right. Before they had finished the first verse
the door creaked open and a stout badger in a smart uniform glared
out at them.

'Go away,' he snarled. 'You've no business to come snooping
round other people's houses. Don't let me catch you here again
until . . .' He stopped suddenly and slammed the door.

The three friends were speechless. 'He didn't give us a chance!' said Willy at last. 'Our singing wasn't that bad.'

'It wasn't the singing,' said Harvey thoughtfully. 'They just don't want visitors. Did you notice all the windows were shuttered?'

'I told you the place gives me the creeps,' said Rue.

'I bet Squire Fox told him to get rid of us,' panted Willy as they ran down the path.

All the way home Willy kept on and on about the squire's meanness. 'He won't go without at Christmas,' he grumbled. 'As long as he's got enough for himself, he'll never think about Foxwood.'

'You're jealous,' said Rue.

'I'm not,' said Willy, 'I just wish my plan had worked, that's all.'

Harvey yawned. 'I don't want anything at the moment,' he said, 'except my bed and no more carol singing.'

'What about taking the toboggans to the woods tomorrow and collecting bundles of firewood to sell,' said Rue.

'Good idea,' said Harvey.

'Don't forget to bring string,' called Willy, as each trudged off wearily to his own home.

The next morning, after a good hot breakfast, the three friends set off for the woods, each pulling his toboggan. Willy's mum had given him a loaf of bread and a flask of soup.

'That will keep you all going,' she said, as she waved him off.

Willy's legs were so short and the snow was so deep that he soon felt tired. Harvey and Rue kindly took it in turns to pull his toboggan and give him a ride on one of theirs. When they reached the wood Rue was all for getting to work at once.

'Shall we eat first?' suggested Willy hopefully. 'Mum has put soup and a fresh loaf in the hamper.'

Harvey and Rue were easily persuaded, so they found a sheltered spot and shared out the picnic.

'I could work all night now,' said Rue happily, when the last crumb had gone.

Harvey, Rue and Willy soon had their toboggans piled high with neatly tied bundles.

'That's the last of the string,' said Rue. 'We'd better be getting home.'

'It should fetch a fair price,' said Willy, already thinking about what he could buy with his share.

The laden toboggans were heavy to pull. By the time they reached the edge of the wood Willy's legs were aching. He was thinking longingly of his earlier rides, when, suddenly, he heard a loud cry.

The cry echoed again through the tall, bare trees.

'Listen,' said Willy. 'I thought I heard someone call "help".'

At that moment they saw a small badger running towards them. 'There's been an accident,' he called breathlessly. 'Please come.'

Harvey, Rue and Willy followed the little badger out of the wood. Suddenly Willy stumbled on a snow-covered log and landed in front of a carriage that had skidded off the road, and was hanging over the edge, above a sheer drop to the icy river below. Two horses stood shivering in the shafts.

'Is anyone hurt?' gasped Willy, as the others came hurrying up.

A tall fox appeared from behind the carriage, dusting the snow from an expensive-looking coat. 'We're unharmed but a little shaken,' he said calmly.

Rue freed the horses, while Harvey comforted the coachman. Willy wanted to know what had happened.

'Icy roads,' said the fox. 'The horses slipped on a bad patch and before we knew what was happening the coach was half over.'

The coachman scratched his head. 'The problem is,' he asked, 'how do we get it back?'

'I think I know,' said Willy. He beckoned to the little Badger. 'Come with me. I'll need help.'

'What's he up to now?' asked Rue.

'I've a horrible feeling I know,' said Harvey a few minutes later, as Willy and his new friend appeared, pulling the three toboggans.

'What are you going to do, Willy?' asked Rue anxiously.

'Use the wood from the toboggans to make planks for the carriage wheels to grip on.'

'But we spent hours making them,' protested Rue, 'and the wood took all our money.'

'I know, but it's the only way,' said Willy firmly.

They set to work, pulling strips of wood from the toboggans and forcing them under the wheels.

'This had better work,' Harvey told Willy, 'or you're for it.'

Everyone worked hard. First they scraped the snow from under the carriage then Willy laid a line of toboggan planks under the wheels. The fox and the coachman brought some strong branches from the wood to use as levers.

When all was ready everyone pushed and heaved till, with one final effort, the carriage stood upright, its wheels resting on the planks. The footman roped the horses to the back, and with much coaxing persuaded them to pull the old coach slowly back on to the road.

'Brilliant, Willy,' said the fox. 'We'd have been stuck without your help.' Then his eye caught the splintered wood lying in the snow. 'Sorry about your toboggans.'

'They were new,' Willy said. 'I don't think Harvey and Rue are very pleased with me.'

'I was on my way to shop in town,' went on the fox briskly. 'Hop aboard, everybody, and we'll mix business with pleasure. It seems I've one or two things to add to my shopping list.'

'There's no point in our coming,' said Harvey. 'We've no money. That's why we were collecting wood to sell.'

'We wouldn't mind the ride, though,' said Willy quickly.

When everybody had settled down, the fox said suddenly, 'Your little friend's going off.'

'We don't know him,' said Rue. 'We thought he was with you. He raised the alarm, so he's the one you really ought to thank.'

The fox jumped down, ran after the little badger and, after a few minutes talk, they came back together.

As they drove into town they discovered their
new friend's name was Jeremy, that his parents were dead,
and that he lived on his own in the wood.

'You must be very lonely,' said Willy. 'Why don't you come and
live with us? My mum won't mind, and anyway you're too small to
eat much.'

Jeremy smiled. 'Thanks,' he said.

'This is great,' said Harvey happily, as the carriage bowled along. 'Now I know what it feels like to be a prince.'

The fox was enjoying himself too. 'How about singing some carols?' he suggested. 'After all, it is Christmas.'

'Don't talk about carols,' muttered Willy. 'We went to sing carols to the squire at the Manor House yesterday. He's horribly mean, not a bit like you. His butler slammed the door in our faces.'

The fox smiled. 'Not all foxes are mean, you know.'

'Oh, I didn't mean that,' said Willy blushing, 'but . . .'

'Just keep quiet, Willy,' said Rue, 'you've said enough.'

When they reached the town, the fox gave them some money for Christmas shopping. 'I've got some business to do,' he said. 'We'll meet at the old tea rooms at 5 o'clock.'

The four friends looked at the money in their hands and then at each other. 'We'll be able to buy an awful lot with this,' said Rue, breaking the silence.

'Let's split up,' said Harvey. 'Some of my presents are secret.'

'O.K.,' said Willy, guessing one of them might be for him. 'But I'll keep Jeremy with me in case he gets lost.'

The fox was the first to arrive at the old tea rooms, and he had already ordered by the time Willy arrived, followed by Rue and Harvey.

'Where's Jeremy?' asked Rue as they sat down.

'We got separated in one of the shops,' said Willy, looking rather sheepish. 'I didn't look for him because I thought he would come straight here.'

'It's getting dark,' said the fox, 'so I'd better go and find him. You three stay here, eat your tea, and don't wander off.'

'That fox bothers me,' said Harvey, as they ate their scones. 'Why haven't we seen him before?'

'He's rich and he's generous,' said Willy.

'But where does he live?' asked Harvey.

'Well, rich people live in large houses,' said Rue.

'Precisely,' said Harvey. 'Manor houses!'

Willy choked on his teacake. 'You mean he's Squire Fox,' he gasped. 'And I went on about the Squire being miserable and mean. I never thought . . . What am I going to do?'

At that moment the fox returned, carrying a very tired Jeremy. 'I found him fast asleep under the Christmas tree in the square,' he said. 'Eat up now, it's getting late and I want to get you all safely home.'

Willy stood up and faced the fox. 'Sir,' he said bravely, 'or rather, Squire. I have some apologising to do. I didn't mean to call you names, and I had no idea you were the new Squire. You are, aren't you?' he added hastily.

'You're forgiven, Willy,' smiled the Squire. 'And I've got some explaining of my own to do. I'll tell you all about it on the way home.'

On the way back to Foxwood Squire Fox stopped the carriage and everyone picked holly and mistletoe for the Manor House.

'What a splendid squire he is,' said Willy as he and Jeremy walked home.

'One of the best,' agreed Jeremy.

'And what a surprise his news will be to the village,' said Willy. 'I don't know how we'll keep the secret till tomorrow. Come on, Jeremy,' he finished. 'Let's introduce you to my mum.'

Willy's mother watched them from the kitchen window, struggling up the path with armfuls of parcels.

'Hi, Mum,' said Willy as she opened the door. 'This is Jeremy.'

'Come in and welcome, Jeremy,' said Mrs Hedgehog. 'Warm yourselves by the fire while I get the supper, then I want to hear what you've been up to all day, Willy, and how you met Jeremy.'

But supper came too late. Willy and Jeremy fell asleep by the warm fire and Mr Hedgehog carried them up to bed.

Next morning, Willy shook Jeremy awake. 'Christmas Eve,' he said. 'The day we wrap up all our presents and put them under the tree.'

'Great,' said Jeremy. 'A real family Christmas.'

Mrs Hedgehog heard this remark. 'I hope you'll enjoy being with us, Jeremy,' she said. 'And stay as long as you want.'

While they were eating breakfast the town crier came by. 'Oh yez! Oh yez!' he called. 'The new squire invites everyone to a Christmas Eve Fancy Dress Party at the Manor House. 5.30 sharp!'

'Hurray,' shouted Willy. 'The secret's out.'

'You mean you know about this, Willy,' gasped his mother. 'And you managed to keep the secret.'

'It's a long story,' said Willy, 'and there's no time to tell you now because we've got to get our costumes ready.'

The whole evening was a huge success. There were party games, prizes and sleigh rides round the grounds.

The food and drink were so good that Willy soon
had to admit that he couldn't eat any more.

At the end of the evening the Squire had two surprises left. He called Harvey, Rue, Willy and Jeremy outside. There in the snow stood a wonderful toboggan big enough for four.

'It's yours,' he said, 'you've earned it.'

He turned to Jeremy. 'It's no good having a share in the toboggan if you're not here. So what do you say to coming to live with us at the manor house?'

'Agreed,' shouted Harvey, Rue and Willy together.

Jeremy smiled, and nodded happily.